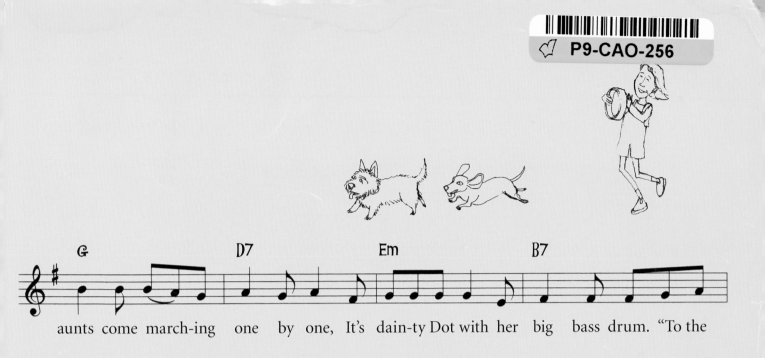

G   **D7**   **Em**   **B7**

aunts come march-ing one by one, It's dain-ty Dot with her big bass drum. "To the

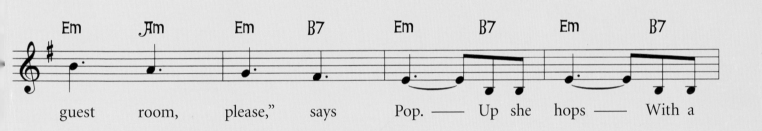

Em   **Am**   **Em**   **B7**   **Em**   **B7**   **Em**   **B7**

guest room, please," says Pop. —— Up she hops —— With a

Em   **B7**   **Em**   **B7**

Thump ———— And a Whump Bump, Bump, Flump.

THIS BOOK
BELONGS TO

....

There is nothing more **FUN** than learning how to read.

Reading takes you on new **ADVENTURES** and helps
you learn new things.

The people of British Columbia want to give you the
GIFT OF READING as you start out in school.

BRITISH
COLUMBIA
The Best Place on Earth | ReadNow BC

THE AUNTS COME MARCHING

BILL
RICHARDSON

ARTWORK BY
CYNTHIA NUGENT

RAINCOAST BOOKS

Vancouver

To music teachers everywhere — march on!
BILL RICHARDSON

For Frank Ludwig, my favourite singing conductor
CYNTHIA NUGENT

Raincoast Books gratefully acknowledges the ongoing support of the Canada Council for the Arts, the British Columbia Arts Council and the Government of Canada through the Book Publishing Industry Development Program (BPIDP).

Edited by Grenfell Featherstone
Cover and interior design by Teresa Bubela

Library and Archives Canada Cataloguing in Publication

Richardson, Bill, 1955–
The aunts come marching / Bill Richardson; artwork by Cynthia Nugent.

ISBN 978-1-55192-990-3 (BOUND)
ISBN 978-1-55192-872-2 (PBK.)

1. Musical instruments—Juvenile fiction.
2. Picture books for children.
1. Instruments de musique—Romans, nouvelles, etc. pour la jeunesse.
2. Livres d'images pour enfants.
I. Nugent, Cynthia, 1954–
II. Title.

PS8585.I186A95 2007   JC813'.54   C2006-905235-2

Library of Congress Control Number: 2008934355

Raincoast Books
9050 Shaughnessy Street
Vancouver, British Columbia
Canada V6P 6E5
www.raincoast.com

www.pgw.com

Printed in Canada by Friesens

10 9 8 7 6 5 4 3 2 1

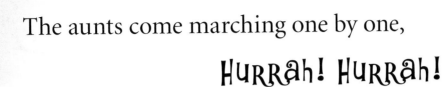

The aunts come marching one by one,

HURRAH! HURRAH!

The aunts come marching one by one,

HURRAH! HURRAH!

The aunts come marching one by one,

It's dainty Dot with her big bass drum.

"To the guest room, please," says Pop.

Up she hops

With a **Thump**

And a **Whump**

Bump,

Bump,

Flump.

The aunts come marching two by two,

HURRAh! HURRAh!

The aunts come marching two by two,

HURRAh! HURRAh!

The aunts come marching two by two,

It's piccolo Pat with sousaphone Sue.

"To the guest room, please," says Pop.

Up they hop

With a HOOT

And a BLOOT
TWEET,
TWEET,
TOOT.

The aunts come marching three by three,

HURRAH! HURRAH!

The aunts come marching three by three,

HURRAH! HURRAH!

The aunts come marching three by three,

They've each got cymbals on their knees.

"To the guest room, please," says Pop.

Up they hop

With a Smash

And a Bash

CRING,
CRING,
CRASH!

The aunts come marching four by four,

HURRAH! HURRAH!

The aunts come marching four by four,

HURRAH! HURRAH!

The aunts come marching four by four,

They blast their trumpets at the door.

"To the guest room, please," says Pop.

Up they hop

With a HONK

And a GRONK

BLam,

BLam,

BLONK.

The aunts come marching five by five,

HURRAH! HURRAH!

The aunts come marching five by five,

HURRAH! HURRAH!

The aunts come marching five by five,

They pump their bagpipes up the drive.

"To the guest room, please," says Pop.

Up they hop

With a SQUEEZE

And a WHEEZE

SNORE, SNORE, SNEEZE.

The aunts come marching six by six,

HURRAH! HURRAH!

The aunts come marching six by six,

HURRAH! HURRAH!

The aunts come marching six by six,

They blow bassoons and do high kicks.

"To the guest room, please," says Pop.

Up they hop

With a Whoosh

And a Moosh

Squawk, Squawk,

Squoosh.

The aunts come marching seven by seven,

HuRRah! HuRRah!

The aunts come marching seven by seven,

HuRRah! HuRRah!

The aunts come marching seven by seven,

With harps as if they've come from heaven.

"To the guest room, please," says Pop.

Up they hop

With a SPRUNG

And a SPROING

PING, PING, POING.

The aunts come marching eight by eight,

HURRAH! HURRAH!

The aunts come marching

eight by eight,

HURRAH! HURRAH!

The aunts come marching eight by eight,

They toot kazoos and juggle plates.

"To the guest room, please," says Pop.

Up they hop

With a HEm

And a Hum

zim,

zim,

zum.

The aunts come marching nine by nine,

HURRAH! HURRAH!

The aunts come marching nine by nine,

HURRAH! HURRAH!

The aunts come marching nine by nine,

Trombones all polished till they shine.

"To the guest room, please," says Pop.

Up they hop

With a **WHEEEEE**

And a **WHaaaaa**

BLOOP, BLOOP,

BLaaaaa.

The aunts come marching ten by ten,

HURRAH! HURRAH!

The aunts come marching ten by ten,

HURRAH! HURRAH!

The aunts come marching ten by ten,

And here's the conductor, Auntie Gwen.

"To the guest room, please," says Pop.

Up she hops.

He looks glum

When the drum

Whum,

Whum,

Pums.

When all the aunts begin to play,

HURRAH! HURRAH!

When all the aunts begin to play,

HURRAH! HURRAH!

When all the aunts begin to play,

Then Pop hops up to march away.

"And I won't come back," says Pop,

"Till they STOP

With the Thump

And the Bump

CRING CRING PING PING

Blam Blam Bliff Bloof

Blaaaaaast!"

PEACE
AT
LAST.

The Aunts Come Marching

Em ..... G

1. The aunts come march-ing one by one, Hur-rah! —— Hur-rah! —— The

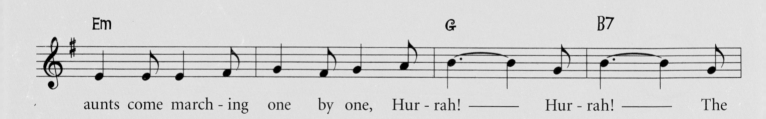

Em ..... G B7

aunts come march-ing one by one, Hur-rah! —— Hur-rah! —— The